The Floating Cemetery
Author And Illustrations

By: John Sylvester Sr

@ 2020 Copyrights. All rights reserved. No part of this book may be reproduced, stored in a retrieval system or transmitted in any form or by any means without the prior written permission of the publisher. Except a review may "brief passage in every view to be printed in a newspaper magazine or journal."

This book is totally fiction and any persons or places are coincidental to the story or events. The characters are a figment of imagination and the incidences described in each chapter are fake.

This story was written for entertainment and enjoyment purposes only. This book does not entertain anyone performing the acts portrayed.
They are dangerous and should not be attempted or duplicated.

ISBN: 9798647818836

Dedication

This book is dedicated to my readers and Derek Kaczmarczyk . He is employed at the New Lenox Police Department. Derek is an officer of unforgettable performance. I will always remember him for the help he extended me on March 25, 2020. I thank you.

My appreciation is also extend to Dans Towing located in New Lenox, Illinois. They went above the call of the honor and dignity to help me. They were called by Derek to resolve a problem with my truck.

What they did was unforgettable. The man spent 25 minutes helping me and didn't charge me a dime. These are two angels in the dedication of this book. Bless both of you.

This is my fifth book and I hope every reader enjoys it. Thank you.

Synopsis

It's a pleasure to see you back again. I know " The Floating Cemetery" will bring hours of enjoyable reading. The beginning starts with two Afro-American brothers from Indianapolis. They went to Las Vegas, Nevada to find their mother.

To give you some background on these men. They are from Indianapolis and grew up with a single Mother. Their grandmother raised them while the Mother worked. She was a nurse in the hospital.

They were street gang related and hung with ghetto rough people. The streets taught them mean and heartless acts that caused misfortune in many lives.

(Update From The Prior Book). Their Mother Amy Black is a

50-year-old African-American female. She was not married and was just released from prison. She served several years in the Indiana Woman's penitentiary.

She's been missing for a month and a half. Her two sons haven't heard from her. Emily Black, her Mother filled a missing persons report in Indiana.

It's been six months and not a word from the police

department. The covert 19 virus was starting to hit the nation. President Trump issued a no movement order over the entire country.

It wasn't possible for her to go look for Amy. She needed to find her so she hired a private detective. His name was Scott Taylor. He came from the Taylor Detective agency. He served on different departments in the last twenty years. He retired and opened his own agency.

He traced Amy and her two sons to Las Vegas, Nevada. Unknown to him he discovered a series of murders involving different people. You could read more stories of Amy black and her disappearance in my third book,

"The Case Of Amy Black."

Amazon.Com. ISBN: 978-1-71615-038-8

This story is about people involved in her disappearance. Taylor cracked the case but had a very difficult task doing it. The Black Brothers snitched on two murders. A price is put on their their heads by the Thrill Killers. Discover the outcome in the pages of this manuscript .

(Act1). I'm going to address the Black Brothers by their street names. We'll call them Britt T. and Earl Q. These two brothers are in their 20s. Britt T is 25 and Earl Q is 23 yrs. Old.

They both have a muscular build. They are dark- skinned Afro Americans, Jamaican in blood. Their hair is short. One wears a low Afro cut and the other wears a collegian style cut.

These gentlemen are always well-dressed with the latest accessories. Their bling consists of gold around their necks and on their fingers. These boys have accomplished great things on the streets of Indianapolis. They were involved in drugs and weren't street punks.

It was hard for them growing up. Their father left their mother when they were young . The mother worked all her life. The grandmother couldn't hold control on them. They were terrorizing the streets of Indianapolis as teens.

They became involved with gangs for protection. The neighborhood was very rough with fights, stabbings and shootings.

They admit facing difficult problems growing up. Their Mother and Grandmother are very proud of them. They didn't agree with their activities but they turned into strong men.

During their lives every Sunday their Grandmother took them to a Christian church. They were raised Christian and saved by the blood of Jesus.

Without the consideration of their faith they were monsters. Things they were involved in were unacceptable to their faith.

(Act11). We're going to revisit a past episode that happened between the Black brothers and Sandra Burns.

This is her first encounter with the Black brothers. She took the elevator to the garage. It was located below the main building. She exited the elevator and seen two man following her.

The gentleman were well dressed. She could hear the footsteps behind her.

She arrived at your car and open the door. Once inside she started it. She noticed the strangers coming towards her. She put the car in drive and sped out of the parking lot. The two males chased the car by foot to the exit.

Sandra was petrified because she didn't know who the hell was following her.She picked up her cell phone and called Seth Oleo.

He was another a Doctor involved in the murder of Amy black. She told Seth," I'm being followed! She went on explaining how. She explained how they were waiting for her ad how frightened she became.

Seth told her to go home and he would call the police. He would meet her at the house.

Sandra drove straight home and as she arrived there was a squad sitting in front.

They had arrived before her. She pulled into the lot and parked. The officer walked up to her and open the door. As she stepped out he asked, " Are you Sandra Burns?"

" Yes! I'm happy you're here, I'm scared to death. So scared it's sickening me." She told the officers.

"What's the problem?" The officer asked.

I was being followed by to black men. I drove away from them rapidly and lost them. The exit gate closed as I drove out, It's stopped them. They were on foot in the garage chasing after me." She explained .

"Let's get inside and I'll take a report. You'll be getting a case number and my business card when I leave here. Let's go!"

The officer told her. They followed behind her as she walked up the stairs .

"Did you get a good look at these men?" The officer asked Sandra.

"All I remember is two black gentleman. They looked in their early 20s. About 5' 9" tall. Both of them were dark skinned but one was a little bit lighter.

They wore bluejeans with white gym shoes and hoodies. That's all I could see as I sped out of the gate. I noticed their clothing from the rearview mirror." She answered.

In the meantime Seth had arrived. She let him in and he sat down by the door. He didn't say anything he just sat and listened.

 The officers asked for a few more questions to complete the investigation. They told her they will be back with a copy of the report. A few minutes pasted and a officer knocked at the door. When she opened it he handed her the report.

They left assuring her she would have no more problems. If she sees them again to call their office.

Sandra was so scared she went home with Seth. The two of them relax from the event. The next day the a private detective phoned her. He made an appointment to visit with her. His name was Scott Taylor- Taylor Agency. He arranged to meet her at 5 PM. At her home.

That evening they meet as planned. He introduced himself and she offered him a drink. He sat in a chair nearest the window. The window overlooked the main drag. She was walking around with a drink in her hand and speaking of the encounter. He had a ledger and was writing down her comments.

"Mrs Burns, I was handed your information from the officer that was here last night. I wanted to tell you those men were the sons of Amy Black. They are the called the Black brothers. They go by the name Mr ZQ and Big T. They are members of a gang out east in Indianapolis.

I understand you were associated with their mother.

Her name is Amy. She came down here for some type of job interview. She was supposed to met with you according to her mother. She's disappeared and I'm looking for her. What can you tell me about her?" He asked.

Sandra was surprised to hear who the men were. She knew they had visited with her in Crossville. She didn't want to tell Scott the truth about Amy.

As Scott continued investigated the Amy black story he stood up. He happen to look out the window and noticed a green sedan sitting out front with two black males. He didn't say anything to Sandra. He didn't want to scare her. He knew it was the same man. If they see him go out the door they might follow him. That would be perfect if it would get them away from the building. He could ditch them down the road. Scott excuse himself.

He said, " I'll be back in touch! Goodbye". Then walked out the door.

He walked down the stairs and thru the hallway. He opened the door and left. The two gentlemen stared at him from the car. He walked around his car ignoring them and got him. He started it and pulled away. They turn the lights on and followed him.

Scott was able to speed away. They did just as he wanted followed him away from the residence. He drove an old cop cruiser with a big V-8. They had a small rental with a six. They couldn't keep up with him.

Scott made it back to the motel. He pulled in the parking lot and got out. As he was walking to his room the sedan appeared. It came at a high rate of speed over the sidewalk almost hitting him.

The passenger or Q started shooting at him. They shot the windows out of his cruiser. Scott stood up and fire back. The back window was blown out of their sedan.

They left the garage and sped away. He knew it was the Black brothers. He has positively identified them.

Due to the virus the streets were empty in Vegas. It was easier for Scott to walk around and spot the Blacks car. He knew the Black brothers were severely dangerous . He had to investigate Amy's disappearance. The job was becoming much harder than he had anticipated.

Things were quiet in the morning. Scott got up and went downstairs for breakfast. He walked down the street and arrived in front of the casino. He knocked on the door and Seth came to invite him in. He locked the door behind him. He had a conversation with him about Amy.

Seth when on telling him about Amy. What the police had knew about her and how she disappeared. During that time the Black brothers were questioned but before they could locate Amy's body the Black brothers were arrested.

They did a short bit but have since been released. The information I wrote about was from the past books. Seth is now in prison and Sandra is dead. She died from the coronavirus in Moline, Illinois where the two of them relocated.

The Black brothers have terrorized Moline . This is where the story picks up. They went there seeking Seth and Sandra. Sandra Burns had plastic surgery. Her real name was Millie Franklin. I know it sounds confusing but she died as Sandra Burns. The black brothers wanted to get justice for their mother. They were seeking them for revenge. They found out they were either in jail or dead. That news was disappointing to the Black brothers. They went out of the police station in a rage.

To survive they began robbing stores and selling hard drugs. People would walk down the street and the brothers would hit them in the head and take their wallets and cell phones.

They would take anything that could bring them some cash. Easy pawn items were their goal and they were good at it. They are survivors and the streets of Indianapolis thought them to wrong. They were willing to get rich but not to get right as their Christian upbringing thought them.

The Black brothers were unaware of Shawn and Earl. They were the two thugs that worked for Seth. They were in the penitentiary but heard the Black brothers were in Moline.

They arranged for a hitch their heads. The black brothers were going to get what they had coming. With the news of the Blacks came Jack Bianchi. He was a hitman for the old mob in Chicago.

Act (111). Jack Bianchi didn't care about his background only about money too be made make. He has $5000.00 coming for the heads of the Black brothers. He was about to earn every penny.

One of the requirements for payment was, " He submit pictures of the beheaded bodies."

We're going to take a walk back in time. I want to give

you a biography of Jacks past. We're going to go back to Chicago 1956. Jack was born in April of that year. He was the last of five and had a brother and sister older than him.

The mother was a beautiful sweet lady. She raised them with help from parents.Their names were Nick and Loretta. They originally lived on the north side. He was a taylor had a shop downtown with six

clerks. He had several stores throughout the 20s.
One day a man came into the store demanding protection money. Nick refused to pay them for protection. He would go to work with a gun rolled up in the newspaper. The old man was tough.

That day the mob member walked into the store he sat in a chair. He ordered a Taylor made suit and was waiting for a fitting. While he was being measured the gentleman demanded protection money. Nick wasn't intimated to easily. He stood up to the man and threatened back.

"I'm going to sliced your throat if you say one more word about protection. I have a barbers razor in my pocket. Who's gonna protect you right now because I won't hesitate to cut you!"

" Get out!" He demanded!

The man got up and left but months the mob followed him and threatened continually. They through bricks and machine gunned his building and windows.

Worse came to worse he had to give in. But he became acquainted with a lot of them. They loved him because he moved to the southwest side. He bought a brick bungalow. It was actually a shell.

He had to put in the drywall and all the doors and framing . He made a beautiful home for the family. He sold the building on The north side and moved. They lived in the new house for many years until he passed away and it was sold.

During that time he helped raised Jack and the two others. He put Jack through college. He went downtown and attended college during the early 70s. When he graduated he found good jobs in shops thru out the south.

His job matched his image. He was tough and so was his brother Ron. They would raise hell in the neighborhood once the Mother moved out of the parents house. She purchased her own and the kids were on their own as teens.

They would cut school and turn over busses during the riots in the sixties. Everyone hung up in a shopping center after hours.

During gang fights windows were smashed on cars with chains and rivals would submit to terrible beatings. A few arrests but not many because they were smart.

The Mother took a bus downtown in the morning because she had no car. After working for several years she was finally able to buy a used Buick. A big four-door brown and cream colored on top. She loved the car.

Jack pushed a kid down the stairway at the high school. The kid broke his leg and arm while Jack escaped punishment . No one snitched because they were afraid of gang members.

The shopping center he hung at after school is no longer there. During those years he would tore up the streets with his brother and friends. There was a gentleman named Pete that would hang the brother. He was a tough person an between the three of them they were ruthless. Being involved in different criminal activity was their entertainment.

Jack got married and bought a home. He quit the Taylor business after several years. His job downtown with a man he called Rascal paid much better. He caught a gig with a radio station selling air time.

Jack married and was living near Chicago. He went to jail after his divorce. He was there for seven years for burglary .

While he was incarcerated Shawn and Earl contacted him. Through the grape vine of correspondence he accepted a hit on the Black brothers. They knew he was the man for the job.

He was getting out in a few weeks and promised he

would do it without fail. When he was released he rented a car drove directly to Moline. When he arrived the shit hit the fan and let's get in to that!

Just before he left Joliet he picked up a friend named Chucky Bowen. Chucky was about three years older than him. This man was a crackhead and he was ruthless.

He drove down to Moline with Jack and they stayed at a campground. Jack's friend had a camper that he gave to Jack. They lived there for several months before they began to follow the Black brothers. It was the perfect hide out. They parked across the river in Bettendorf Iowa.

It was parked in a privately owned campground west of town that was secluded off Rt.80. The lot rent was cheap and it camp was unknown to many people.

Just to pass the time Chucky was hired on to remodel the bathrooms in the camp. He spent most of the time doing that and drinking beers.

At night the two of them went following the Black brothers. They were determined to learn their habits. The places they visited and the people they were acquainted with.

A piece of information surfaced about their behavior. The Black brothers were running prostitutes in Moline downtown by the waterfront. It was a popular business district accompanied by popular social clubs. It serves as a perfect setting for the women to seduce gentleman.

The ladies were dressed with cheek tight shorts, nylons and stiletto heels. Their hair was done up and their faces were professionally made up.

They would congregate up and down the street. Most men picked them up in Cars near the corner. There were others walking out of the bar looking for sexual pleasures . The ladies were working and working hard.

There wasn't too much going on in Davenport. The Davenport police heavily patrolled that side of the river. There was industry on the other side allowing the Johns to conduct their business between the buildings. It was a prostitute hot spot.

A casino located in Davenport was another hotspot for these prostitutes. It was at the casino that Jack and Chucky approached the two prostitutes and made a sexual deal.

They really didn't care about the sex. There was another reason they wanted to get acquainted with the ladies.

They were going to use them to induce the Black brothers to come to them. This was in their plan to nab the two of them. The ladies were otherwise unimportant in the situation.

Chucky and Jack had dated the ladies on several occasions. The ladies believed in them and trusted them. They would make arrangements to meet and the ladies were always on time.

They would show up dressed in their sexiest clothes. They wined and dined these ladies for months. Chucky and Jack questioned them about the black brothers. The girls were very open and didn't hide anything from them.

During the evening one of the ladies asked, " How young they were when they were introduced to the mob?"

 They thought back and Jack started telling a story.

Jack and Chucky were nine years or old ten at the time. They were walking up and down the city street looking for trouble. They begin scratching the cars that were parked with rocks. It didn't take long for them to get caught.

Mr. Rascal came our from one of the houses and caught the boys scratching his car. He grabbed the children by the neck and shook them. He told them they better not come back to his car again. He was going to break their kneecaps and let them go. The boys certainly remembered the image on Mr. Rascals face. He was so mad they were glad he didn't take them to confront the parents.

 The boys went down by the golf course and decided to wade in the little pond. It was full of golf balls they wanted to retrieve. They took off their shoes and socks and waded into the water. The boys would surface the balls and sell them back to the players. It was a way to make a few dollars.

(Act 1V). From afar came a car that stopped as it approach the pond. It was Mr. Rascal and his driver. The two boys hid down by the walkway. The boys kept an eye on both of them. A man was pulled out of the car and giving a severe beating.

When he fell to the ground they kicked and stomped him. The man passed out. The driver picked him up by the neck and dragged him to the waters edge and dumped him in.

They left him in the waters and ran up the hill then took off in their. The two boys started talking.

"Let's go to help him". Jack said.

" I don't think we should get involved with Mr. Rascal. I have to get home." Chucky said.

"No! Thats not fair! I'm not afraid of him. We need to report what he did. Its not right."Jack said.

" Let's go Jack will get in trouble that was Mr Rascal!" Chuck. Replied.

""I'm not going! I want to see how the man is! He could be alive and would appreciate us helping him. That man can't move because they broke his ribs or something ." Jack said.

"Ok! let's go and see how he is!" Chucky said.

They walked down to the riverfront and approached the man. He was moaning and trying to move in the water. He seen the children approaching and told them, "Get out of here ! Get out of here!" With a very angry voice.

The boys didn't say a word as they turned and ran away.

When they arrived back on the street they decided to visit the police department. They walked down the road and arrive at the station.

The boys stood in front of the desk Sergeant and told him what they seen. He didn't believe them and thought they were making it all up.

"A big fib!" He told the boys.

Jack started insisting they believe him. The Sergeant

ordered another cop to go pick up Mr. Rascal. He was also told to pick up Chuck's Father.

In one hour he brought them both back to the Sargent.

" Here they are Sargent as you requested." The Officer said.

"What's going on here Sargent! Why are you holding my son?" The Father asked.

The two boys thought it was cool to be in the police station. They were proud of themselves. Mr. Rascal was looking at them with bullets is his eyes. He was very upset the two children told on them.

What made it worse is they drag him in front of the Sargent. The Sargent was a good friend of his. He looked at the boys and said, "Are you sure it was me that you seen?" He asked.

Both of the boys shook their head and look towards Chucky's father. They weren't scared to snitch out Mr Rascal.

Jack said to the sergeant. "I think Mr. Rascal was just saying it wasn't him because we had an encounter with him earlier. So he thinks we're just snitching on him to get him in trouble. But it was him!"

The sergeant looked at Mr. Rascal and told him,

" I don't believe these boys! They are just mad at you. You can leave Rascal you're free to go."

" You take these boys home and keep them in the house. I don't want any more trouble from either one of them. Now go! Get out of here!" He explained.

Mr. Rascal went up to Jack and gave him a ten dollar bill. He told him to come by his house the next day. He wanted to talk to the two boys. They did as he instructed.

The next day the two boys went by his house. Mr. Rascal told them they could be his eyes. They had to keep an eye on his house and his car. He would pay them every week. As the boys grew up they became gangsters. This was all at the hands of Mr. Rascal. He began to love the young men.

The two ladies were impressed with the story. The two gentlemen sat and giggled about it. They looked at each other and shook their heads remembering how they grow up. Jack stood up and told the girls that he's going to take them back to the riverfront. They had things to do. They drove back to the river and the ladies got out.

Jack and Chucky drove over to the shipyards. Chuck had a friend that worked there in the evenings. He wanted to discuss some things with him. As they pulled up he noticed him. He rolled down the window and yelled, "Hey Ryan!"

Ryan waved back at them and walked over. The two men got out of the car shook hands with him.

"Ryan we need you to do a job for us. "Jack said.

"What do you want? What is it you need?" Ryan asked.

"We'll need you to make something that you could stick four bodies into . Somewhere on the bottom of a Barge. Or one of these barges would do!. That way when the barge is lowered into the water after time they would disintegrate." He said to Ryan.

"That is such a cool idea! Who came up with that?He asked Chuck

Chuck looked Ryan and said, " We have something to take care of for somebody. There's $1500 in it for you. Can you do it?" Chuck he asked.
 Ryan looked at them and laughed.

 "You guys are serious. He said.

 Jack and Chuck looked back and said, "Yes we are. We need it done soon."

"OK ! I could do that. There's an old barge down the way. They snatched it out of the water about a week ago. I can work and that. It will be put on that barge. They're going to be taking that down river soon. It'll be ready for you in a couple weeks. I'll get back to you when I'm finished." Ryan said.

They all shook on the deal and assured Ryan he would have the money once he completed the job. Jack and Chucky got back in the car and left.

(Act V).   It was a ride to the river edge to pick up Sarah. She was one of the prostitutes that work for the Black brothers. She had agreed to a dinner with them and drinks.

That wasn't Jacks motivation with her. to be with them so He was set on talking about the black brothers with her. They had a plan put together in their minds to capture them.

Sarah was waiting at the River walk as she planned. They pulled up and she open the back door. She sat down on the seat and closed the door. Jack turned around and looked at her.

"Sarah you are looking nice today!" He told her.

 "Thank you Jack! You're not look too bad yourself!." She replied.

Chuck was driving. He just turned around and looked at her with a smile. He was a very quiet person. He never really talked. Jack was the mouth piece. He was a follower.

Jack told him to go to the casino. He wanted to eat in a restaurant inside. He drove across the river to Davenport. They arrived at the Casinos entrance. They pulled in the parking lot and gave the attended the car. They use the valet parking which made it much easier.

They pulled up and stoped at the entrance. They got out and walked through the building. They arrived at the restaurant and sat down at a table.

The first thing Jack did was reach in his pocket and pull out a crisp one hundred dollar bill. He handed it to Sarah and said , "This is for you for the evening."

"Thank you Jeff that's more than enough." She excepted the money and put it in her purse. She looked up with a smile at the two of them.

Chucky looked at her and asked," Did you have a wonderful day?"

"It was an average day. Made a lot of money. That's all I care about." She replied.

"Could you put us in touch with one of the black brothers? Jack asked.

"All I Gotta do is pick up the phone." She replied.

"That's great I'm going to keep that in mind. What do you feel like eating today. Have a good dinner! How about a steak or some lobster?" Jack asked.

Sounds good. She reviewed the menu and looked at Jack. "I've decided. I will have the steak with a potato. Can you get me a martini please? Excuse me I have to use the ladies room." She got up and walked away from the table.

"I'll take care of it don't you worry." He replied.

While she was gone Jack and Chuck had a conversation.

"We could get her to tell us about these guys. She should

know a lot about them. Where they live and who they hang with. All their contact names and addresses. Also the clubs that they work. This girl is a pocketbook of information Jack. We need to get it out of her tonight. Let's see what she has to say when she comes back." Chuck told him.

"Don't look now but she's on her way back. I'll start the conversation." Jack said.

They both became silent as she approached the table and sat down.

"That wasn't bad it wasn't too busy in there. I wanted to refresh my make up but the mirrors were all being used. I don't have any more appointments for tonight so I guess I'm ok. What do you think guys?" She asked.

Both of them looked at her and said. "You're always beautiful Sarah. You don't

need any make up. If you were natural you would even look better".
They commented .

"Sarah asked a very unusual question. "Did you guys hear about that robbery at the Brick Rock Company?"

"You're sure on top of things". Jack commented.

"The reason I asked was because I know who did it." She replied.

"Really." He said.

"Sure do! Your two favorite people Jack. They heisted $85,000. Those two boys are rolling in dough plus they have all the ladies working. Isn't that pathetic." She asked?

"Where did you get that bit of information Sarah?"
Jack asked?

"I have my sources Jack. All the girls are talking about it. They're really pissed off these guys are taking their money and they already have so much." She told him.

"I got an idea Sarah. How would you like to dig into their pocket? I have the perfect plan to break them. Want to go for it? What do you think?" He asked her.

"Cool daddy I'm in!" She reply.

He sat quietly for a minute. Chucky looked at him kind of funny and raised his eyebrows. The silence covered the table as Jack was thinking.

"I got it! You're going to call them. Tell them that we went half the money. You're not gonna tell them who we are. You just tell them brothers of the Thrill killers. Threaten them with going to the police." He said.

"That's a cool idea! Thats almost $43,000. Three-way split guys?" She asked.

"Why not! Its not our money anyhow. Wouldn't you like to have a couple thousand dollars in your purse just for talking to them? That's the only way you have to be involved being a mouthpiece!" He commented.

"That's a great idea Jack I have to give it to you. You come up with some smart ones. If we had to put pressure on them this will work. Tell them we will kill one girl a week until they give it to us. That will get their asses moving. All three of them laughed." Chuck had the ideal idea.

"You hit that right on the head Chucky." Jack commented. He turned and looked at Sarah. She laughed.

"That is out of this world. Would you guys really do that?" She asked.

"Hell yeah! You think we're playing with these guys? It's been done before. Its nothing to us. They're just bodies. I want that money. You're going to get busy girl!" He told her.

"Waiter! Get us another round here please. Bring the lady another what she wants."Jack said.

"Martini please!" Sarah said.

Will take a couple of beers guys. The conversation continued. They spoke right through dinner about the plan and agreed they would put it in effect.

Sarah agreed to take them back to her motel room. They didn't want to wait. She was going to call them tonight. The demand for the money was coming. The threat to kill the ladies was going to be told to them.

Jack called for the check and paid the waiter. The three of them walked up to her room at the casino. She was laughing and joking and very calm. Jack walk behind the two of them.

"Once they were in the room they sat on the bed. Ok Sarah! This is going to an act. Let's see how good you are. Do you know what you're going to tell them?" Jack asked.

"I got it jacket. Couldn't be any clearer. To facts! Money and murder. That's about it!" She told him.

"You're just too good Sarah. Ok let's do it! Are you ready Chucky?." Jack asked.

Chucky just looked at him and smiled. He shook his head each way. He sat there not saying one word. This was all Jacks idea.

"Pick up the phone Sarah. Let's get busy and do this. Everybody keep it quiet now! Sarah did and he requested. She took the phone out of her purse and dialed Bretts number. The phone rang about eight times before he answered.

"Brett this is Sarah". She said.

"What do you need girl? Are you making money for me tonight? I'm gonna be picking you up in a little while. I booked you another appointment. What time could you be ready?" He told her.

"I'm not gonna be ready Brett. There's no more work for you. I'm being held by these two men. They forced me to tell them about the robbery you committed. They want half the money. If you don't give them half the money they're going to kill one prostitute a week until it's paid. Don't push them! They might take it all. He wants to talk to you." She told him.

Brett was in shock. He didn't know how to respond to her request. Bert was in the room and Brett looked over at him. Bert happened to notice the shocked look on his face. He silently whispered "What's up?"

Jack grabbed the phone from Sarah. He put it by his mouth and said.

"You heard what the lady said! You have 24 hours to get back to me. Your answer better be what I expected. The first one will die tomorrow. Get that half of the money. $42,000 in a briefcase!" He told Brett.

Brett didn't say anything. He just hung up the phone. Jack laughed.

"This guy thinks I'm playing with him. You're going to call

him tomorrow about 1 o'clock in the afternoon. If he don't have that money the first girl would be dead by 9 o'clock !" Jack told her.

Write his number down for me Sarah. We're going to be split now. Will be back here tomorrow about 11:30 in the morning. Will take it out from there and see if they took what I said seriously .

She took out a pen from her purse and wrote his number down from her cell phone. She handed the slip of paper to Jack. He folded it and put it in his wallet. They grab their coats. Jack and Chuck walked out the door. They said their goodbyes as she closed it.

The gentleman rode back to the trailer at the campground and rested up for the night. They would be back at Sarah's door at 11:30 tomorrow morning. That was the plan.

They were both laughing and talked on the way back.

They both settled in for the night inside the trailer. When morning came they rose from their beds. They both took a shower and dressed. They were on their way back to Sarah's room when they received a call from Brett.

"I want to know who the hell this is? Just to let you know I have Sarah. She's going to get a severe beating for talking to you. I don't have any money and I didn't do anything to get any money! Got it!" Brett told him?

 Brett, if you put one hand on her you're going to give us all the money. Don't give me no bullshit you didn't do the robbery! I know you did! Now you have till 9 o'clock tonight to have a suitcase with half that money packed in it. The first girl dies at 9:30 you got it?

If you wanna know who this is did you ever hear of the thrill killers.? We are their buddies. How's that for a stick in your ass. 9 o'clock tonight Brett. I'll call you. He hung up the phone.

Jack started laughing out loud. He looked at Chucky and said. "This asshole thinks I'm playing with them".

"That's a real joke."Chucky replied.

"The First Lady dies at 9:30. We're going to pick her up and shoot her in the head. Then she is going to be dropped her off in front of his house. In a week will do the same thing . He'll give us that money once he gets the first stiff in front of his door. We're going to put the cops right in his face. That's what I want." Jack said.

"This is the best pressure you could apply!" Chucky told Jack.

The conversation between Bert and Brett wasn't as pleasant. They took Sarah by the neck and started to strangle her. They punched her in the face a couple of times. They wanted information about these guys. She wouldn't tell them anything.

They severely beat her and threw her out into the street. She laid there until the ambulance picked her up.

They broke three ribs and her jaw. She was admitted into the hospital .

Jack and Chucky were notified about the beating she was subjected too .

"Jack called Brett and told him. "I want all the money. I warned you if you hurt her we were taking different measures . Brett, we're going to make sure we enforce that. You'll see!" He hung up the phone.

Jack and Chucky were very upset about Sarah's meeting. They went down to the river walk and confronted a prostitute. She was familiar with them so it wasn't too hard to get her in the car. Jack drove directly to Brett's house. Chucky took a carving knife from the glove box. He turned around and stabbed the lady in the abdomen. They drove up to Bretts place and dumped her in front of the house.

(Act V1). Brett and Bert we're just laying around the house being lazy. The phone calls from Jack didn't upset them. They were conversing about Sarah and I how they beat her because she betrayed them. It wasn't soon after they were talking they heard sirens outside the door.

Ambulances and police Sirens alerted them. They were out in front of the house at the street. The two of them stood up and looked out the picture window of the house. There was a prostitute shot the back lying dead at the curb.

Bert and Britt looked shocked. "He wasn't kidding. There's a whore in front of the house! He dumped the bitch like he threatened. That still don't convince me to give them our money. What do you think Burt? " Brett asked.

"I don't think we should give in so soon. Let's see how far

their willing to take this. If he dumps five more whores in front of the house the police are going to knock on the door. That's when we'll have to get serious about settling with him. Don't give them a dime. They are bluffing."Bert told Brett.

"I don't think so but what do we have to lose. She ain't my daughter or lady. It's just a couple hundred dollars every week because she's not there doing work anymore. We can replace her real easy. You're right we are not taking the bait". Bert laughed.

"They expect us to be on the phone right now calling them. They want us to be scared like little children. I waiting to see what's going to happen. I don't give a hell.

Let them throw as many whores as they want out in front of the house. I'm not going to give in. Let's see what happens next. It's going to take a few days before they do it again. Let's see how serious they are." Brett said.

"It's your call Brett. It really don't matter to me one way or another. I'm with you."Bert said.

It wasn't too long after they completed their conversation there was a knock at the door. Bert went and opened the door. There were three policeman standing on the stoop. One of them step forward and said, "You know this lady out here?" He asked.

"I don't know nothing about what happened out there. Let me put my coat on and I'll come and look. I'll see if I can recognize her. There's no reason why I should know her. If you give me a few minutes I'll be right with you. Bert closed the door went to get his coat.

Before Bret could grab's coat that was another knock at the door. Brett went and answered it.

"He'll be right with you." Brett said.

" Leave the door open. I want to be able to see what he's doing. I believe the two of you had something to do with this lady being dead. I know you're running whores uptown. We're doing an investigation so leave the door open." The Officer told him.

No problem Brett told the officer then walked away from the door. Shortly after words Bert walked up and went outside to where the corpse was lying in the street.

The police took the sheet off from over her face . Bert looked at her knowing who she was. He didn't say anything. "I don't know this woman never seen her before she told the officer."

"Are you sure you don't know her?"The policeman asked.

" I've never seen her like I said." Bert replied.

" Ok! that's what we wanted to know. Thank you! You can go back in the house." The officer instructed.

Bert turned around and went back in the house. He close

the door behind him and looked at Brett.

"This is serious Brett. We need to do something to stop this." Bert said.

"Why don't you call this guy and see what we can work out. I really don't want to do anything with this guy but he's going to keep killing our ladies. We can't have that it's to much heat". Brett told him.

"Well? You have the guys number give him a call and see what you can do." He said.

Brett found the number on the table. Bert had written it on a pad of paper. Brett pick up the phone and dialed. The call was answered. It was Jack.

"What can I do for you?" He said.

"Yeah! I receive the package you delivered. "Chuckle"

"Chuckle" wasn't too nice. We need to talk." Brett said to Jack.

"Dude! You know my demands." He replied.

"We have to do a deal. What if we were to give you a third. Would that satisfy you? I could have that together for you this afternoon. Will you accept that?" Brett said to Jack.

"One of you come out to the river walk. I don't want to see both of you. I'll send a messenger to talk to you about the settlement. I wanted you to meet him in the brush near the river edge.

"I mean 5th street. There's a part that is wooded. It's near the boat yard. We will there at 3 o'clock. One of you. If I see both of you I won't show up. Understood?" Jack told him then hung up the phone.

"Once Jack completed the phone call with Brett he called the gentleman at the shipyard. He answered the phone and jack asked, " Are my convenience ports ready yet?"

"Yes! They are by the way". He replied.

 "Could we bring you someone today?" Jack asked.

 " Yes! You can about 4:30 pm if that's OK with you. I'll be

waiting at the yard. The workers leave here at four. Don't get here any earlier then 4:30 . I'll be out there. He hung up the phone.

"We can meet him there at 4:30. We will be rid of one of these brothers today. He said the boxes are ready at the bottom of the ship.

This is gonna work out sweet. Will kill the first one at four and the second after we collect all the money. We'll take him to the boat exterminate him. The two of them will be taken down river." Chucky said.

"Cool! This is gonna work out. Let's get ourselves together and drive down to the shipyard. The guy should be about a half a block away. Will go meet him and get him in the car. We will kill him driving to the shipyard. You know what's going to happen home after that." The two of them laughed out loud. He told Jack.

"You're going to have to do that. I don't know if I can stomach that. I'm not even gonna watch."
Chucky told him.

"I really think we should bring him all the way to the shipyard before we kill him. There's gonna be blood all inside the car and I don't want it. I'm sure that Ryan will help us. Will do it that way.

I'll get him in the car and you drive down to the shipyard. I'll keep a gun to his head. He better have some of that money. I'm going to really be pissed that suitcase is empty. Let's get going". Jack said.

"The two of drove down to the river edge by the Riverwalk. It wasn't too far from the shipyard. They sat and waited for the Black boys. It's been about an hour and a car pulled up. Right on time it was 3:55. A gentleman exited the car with a brown suitcase.

He walked back in the woods. When he was out of the car the driver took off. Chucky followed him into the woods. They had never meet so neither one of them knew what the other looked like.

He pulled a gun on the man and told him to walk out of the brush. The guy follow the path out to the car. He was put them in the backseat.

Jack started the car and they drove away. As it were cruising Chucky asked the gentleman. Which brother are you?.

"Sorry to disappoint you but I'm not one of the Black brothers. Why would you think I was a Black brother. They asked me to deliver the suitcase to you! And there is money in it. There it is why don't you let me out. No!

You're going to take a ride with us Chucky said.

I'm really pissed they sent someone else. In the meantime Jack picked up the phone and called Bert. "Why isn't this a Black brother?" Jack asked.

"As long as you get the money it doesn't matter." Burt said.

"Yes it does! Now we have a third-party in on this.

He won't be for long. You're going to be responsible for this man's death Bert". Just hung up the phone.

The men heard Jack tell Bert he was going to dispose of him. The man began begging for his life. Chuck and Jack laughed.

 Chucky told him it'll be all over soon. Jack pulls into the shipyard and Ryan was waiting. Jack got out of the car open the back door. He dragged this guy by the shirt collar to the edge of the water. Chucky took the axe out of the trunk of the car and walk behind them. When they got near the water Chucky lifted the X and swung it. He hit this gentleman right in the middle of the back chopping past the heart and into the rib cage.

The man was dead instantly. They laid him down with his head going towards the water over a tree stump. Jack step down into the water and Ryan took the axe and decapitated him.

The blood drained into the into the river so there was no mess. Jack caught the head and put it next to the body. He took a picture for the a Thrill Killers.
That was part of the payment agreement. Jack was to produce a picture of the deceased decapitated and they would forward his money.

They all lifted the body and walked it over to one of the coffins. It was welded underneath the ship. They open the door and lifted the body and laid it inside. The head was laid on top of the stomach.

The latch door was lifted and closed . A pad lock was put over the opening latch and secured.

"There are only two coffins Ryan! I know that's all I asked you for but there's been complications. Would you please make another one. We might have a third corpse ". Jack told Ryan.

"No problem! I'll make another one!That'll be one thousand dollars more and I'll have it ready for you. You have two days to get these other bodies here. The corpse will start to decay. That smell will bring attention and we don't need to get caught. That's the deadline". Ryan told them.

"We'll meet that deadline Ryan on Friday. That's two days from today." Jack assured him.

Both of them turned and walked to the car. Ryan went back to the waterside. He made sure the mess was cleaned there wasn't any evidence a crime committed. He jumped in his car and left.

Jack called the Black brothers. Brett picked up the call. Jack begin the conversation by saying ;

" The bogeyman took your messenger Brett! Do you understand? I told you to come by yourselves! I must meet you on Friday! You and your brother plus a bag of money! Understand?"

"Where at Jack? We'll be there?" Brett answered.

"The same place, both of you at 2 o'clock! This is your last chance don't be late. Bring the rest of the rest of the money!" Jack threatened.

"We'll be there!" Brett hung up the phone.

Jack meant business when he told Brett his ladies would start disappearing. Jack and Chucky drove out to the boardwalk. They solicited another one of Bretts ladies.

She willingly sat in the car. Her name was Caroline. They drove away after making a deal. Jack handed her the phone. He told her to repeat the following.

"Caroline! Pick up the phone and call Brett. You're going to tell him that you are with us and you are number two. They want their money! Understand?

She looked at Jack and asked; " What do you mean number

two? That's none of your business just say that ." He replied.

Caroline called Brett as requested. The phone rang and Brett Answered.

"Brett this is lady Caroline. I was picked up by Jack thinking they wanted service. Once I sat in the I was handed the phone. I am suppose to tell you-

"I am number two! You would know what they mean. They want their money!" Jack took the phone and hung up.

Chucky drove back to the wooded area. When they arrive they parked the car. They told Caroline to get out. She did as instructed and removed herself from the car. They instructed her to take her panties down and she accommodated their second request.

Both men laid in the backseat and raped her numerous times. It went on for a couple of hours. They were hurting her and beating her. She was screaming as she dug her nails into Bretts face.

While Jack was completing his sexual act he was strangling her and laughing at the same time. He put his hands around her neck and chocked the life out of her. He put his clothes back on after cleaning himself and exited the car.

Jack closed the door leaving her lying on the seat. He sat in the front seat and instructed Chucky;

" Drive to the barge!"They pulled into the ship area and Ryan was walking out in the lot. They beeped the horn and he came over to the car. Chucky rolled down the window and before he could say anything Ryan said;

"I see you have another masterpiece in the backseat."

"Yes we just snatched her." Brett answered.

" Do you think I can get some of that before we take her out?" Ryan said.

Chucky thought Ryans request was sick. He looked at Ryan and said;

"If you want to hit that go ahead. Ryan opened the back

door and satisfied his sick appetite. He had sex with a corpse.

Chucky and Jack looked at each other and laughed. They couldn't believe Ryan would screw a corpse. It was funny as hell to them. They have morbid thoughts and Ryan was just like them. Once Ryan completed his task they dragged her out of the car. She was brought over by the barge.

Ryan lifted her up with a forklift to the coffin welded on the bottom of the barge. Ryan open the hatch as she was pushed inside. Another padlock was used to secure the latch.

While these three were busy with the corpse Burt and Brett were frightened.. They know that Caroline was not coming back. They called Jack's phone and the conversation went as follows;

"Jack this is Brett! I have your money! Don't murder our ladies. I will bring the money to you tonight if you say so! Where can we meet?" He asked.

"No! Not until Friday 2 o'clock like I told you. We'll stop killing your ladies as long as you show up. Two o'clock Friday! If you're not there we're going to take two more of them on Saturday. Do you understand?" He asked.

"I understand with no more to say. You'll see both of us at the meeting place." Brett hung up the phone.

The plot was a success. They accomplish what they said out to do. On Friday 2 o'clock they will have all the money from the robbery. $85,000 and be rid of the Black brothers.

The two of them went back to the trailer and relaxed for the evening. They rolled a joint and Chucky had a few lines of cocaine. Jack drank a few beers and fell asleep.

(Act V11). The next morning came fast as Chucky and Jack slept until sunrise.

Chuck rose first and went into the shower to shave and brush his teeth. He came out and dressed. Jack had woken and did the same.

Both of them were ready to threw their day and collect their money. They drove to a restaurant and breakfast was great.

They talked, laughed and had coffee and pancakes. There was trouble to come before the day was over. They were unaware of what was going to happen.

The Black boys haven't forgotten what they've gone threw. They've been terrorized and their ladies have been killed. Even their top hit man was deceased.

The Blacks had arranged for a couple of gun slingers to go with them. It was 12:30 in the afternoon on Friday as Black brothers went to meet with the two gangsters.

The Black gang members carried shot guns. There were two other members joining them. Four in total going to gun down Chucky and Jack.

Chucky and Jack were walking into a trap. They were sitting in the woods waiting for Brett and Bert to appear. There weren't too many people in the turnaround where they were parked . They could see the entranceway to the park very clearly.

Jack felt uncomfortable sitting there. He started the car and moved to a parking lot across the street. Jack put the car in park and picked up his phone. He called Ryan and asked if he had a back up? Could he bring another car of men with him?

He was feeling uncomfortable about the Black brothers.

He didn't feel comfortable meeting them with all that money. Ryan hired three gun slingers that came along with him.

 "We are loaded up with guns. I'll be pulling into the lot shortly. Where are you parked?" Ryan asked.

Jack told them they were in the Walmart parking lot. The

six of them meet shortly after they spoke. Both cars were waiting for the Black brothers.

 The plan was to sabotage them right in the car. Jack was going to grab the money and takeoff. The other gang members were to drag the bodies to the barge.

Two o'clock came quickly and a sedan pulled into the lot. Jack knew it wasn't Brett and Bert. Brett pulled into the wooded area across the street at the turnaround.

Jack knew they were being set up and had been betrayed again. That pissed him off. Ryan was instructed to stop the car carrying the gangsters. They were to drag the four men out of the car and beat their ass.. He was told to keep them there. Chucky and Jack went threw the woods and grabbed the money and the two brothers. They were going to meet Ryan back at the barge. He was to let the four gangsters go.

Jacks plan was to shoot these two guys execution style. He would decapitate them afterwards. Then load them into the metal coffins welded on the bottom of the barge.

Things went pretty well. Jack thought there was going to be a shoot out. They were able to grab the Black brothers and the money with no problem.

The other four men left after Ryan told them to hit the road. Ryan and his three buddies drove back to the ship area. There was six of them going to execute the Black brothers.

Jack was laughing having a good time. He thought this was a real party an execution party. The Black brothers have met their match and their demise .

Ryan took them over by the water side. "Will do it there."

Jack put his gun to Bretts back and walked them over to a side wall. Brett and Bert were to face the wall with their hands up.

Six men walk behind them and begin shooting. Just as if they were having target practice. The men fell to the ground. It was a bloody mess as each man fired five shots.

Ryan started the forklift and lifted both of them up at one time. He carried them over to the Barge. While they were on the forklift each corpses was decapitated. Ryan put the bodies over the water so the blood would drain out without soiling the area.

Ryan lifted the fork up and Jack snapped pictures of the bodies. The gentleman pushed them into each coffin and the latch was padlocked.

"Job well done!" Jack stated.

He walked over to the car and pulled out the suitcase. He counted out $1000 for each person and paid the men. He put the suitcase back in the car and drove off.

The next morning the shipyard workers lowered the barge into the Mississippi river. It sat there for about four hours. The coffins beneath the barge filled with water as the bodies were floating inside their quarters.

The badge was scheduled to leave at 6 o'clock for the south. Everything was going as planned as it began to rain .

Ryan stood inside and filled out the route sheet. Everyone was quite satisfied with their pay off. They received a generous portion of the money.

As the barge sat in the water the bodies were releasing blood. A red shirt was developing around the bottom of the barge. One of the supervisors noticed it and asked Ryan what was causing the ring of red.

 "It was transmission fluid . It was dumped by mistake last night." He replied.

 The man didn't say anything further about it. He smiled

and walked away. They were lucky it wasn't investigated .

Ryan needed the barge to sail as soon as possible. He went and told the captain there was bad weather ahead and he needed to go. The driver agreed and called his men. Then instructed them to prepare to sail."

The crew was ready and were anxious too depart with the bodies underneath. The crew

had no idea what lied beneath them.
It was a floating cemetery. They were traveling south on the Mississippi River.

Jack and Chucky went back to the campground to grab the trailer. They hooked the trailer on the back of the truck. They took off down route 80 and headed toward Chicago. The take was $77,000 that was in the briefcase case on the backseat. Both of them traveled down the road with a smile.

The first thing on their agenda was to go to the penitentiary and visit the two thrill killers. They collected their instructions and wanted to get paid for the Murders.

There was a campground to the south of 80. They stayed there six days because it was convenient to the south suburbs.

(Act V). Inside the penitentiary the inmates were relaxing watching television. Shawn rose and stood in the phone line to call Jack. It wasn't a long line but it was long enough. There was a long wait but it was worth it. Jack had instructed him to call at 8:30 that evening. They communicated by mail handling their business about the Black brothers.

Shawn arrived to the front of the line. He picked up the phone and dialed Jacks number. It rang three times and Jack answered the phone.

It was the operator asking him to accept a collect call from Shawn. Jack was excepting the call and he answered "yes." The conversation went as follows.

"What's been going on Shawn?." Jack asked.

" Nothing much! I heard you took care of that situation. The story is all over the news. I have to say you did a great job. I don't need the pictures because I know you handled your business. You can go over to Collins street and collect your cash. Joe has it! It's there in cash waiting for you. He will pay you off." Shawn answered.

" That's cool! I'll head out there ! What time are we

supposed to be there?" Jack inquired.

" I'll call him and let him know you'll be there tomorrow at 4:pm. Is that OK?." Shawn told Jack.

"Cool! I'll be there at four. Jack hung up the phone.

Jack walked back into the trailer and told Chucky what Shawn had said. Chucky was pleased about the situation. They were going to pick up there money. They relaxed the rest of the day in the camper. Chucky lit up a joint and they got high.

Jack called the crack man and both of them took a ride to his house. They knocked on the door and picked up a forty dollar bag. They rode back to the camper and loaded a pipe. The night went fast after smoking . Both of them fell asleep. of them fell asleep.

Jack was being a crab the next morning. Chucky was very unsettled and couldn't relax. The crack really played with both of them. They both dressed and went to a restaurant for breakfast. After eating breakfast they took off towards Collins street.

There was a three hour wait before they could meet Moe. It was 1 o'clock in the afternoon and they had no other plans for the day .

Time was passing slowly as they sat in front of the Collins street address. While they were sitting talking a car pulled up on the other side of the street. It was the same gangsters that were with the Black brothers in Moline.

The two gentlemen exited the car and went up to the door. They knocked on the door and they were allowed to go in. They were in there quite a while and hadn't come out.

Jack and Chucky got curious as to why they were in there so long. They exited the car and snuck around the house. The two of them looked through the windows. They noticed Moe was being held at gunpoint and they had to do something to help him. Jack wasn't gonna stand around and lose his money. These two characters needed to die. They went back to the car and made a plan to execute both of them.

Chucky remember an entrance to the basement in the back. He would have to go down the stairs. It was an old wooden door. That particular door was never locked and no one used it. It went into the center of the room. The stairs allow them access to the upstairs. The stairway lead to the kitchen in the back of the house.

The plan was to go thru the door and go up the stairs to the kitchen. The plan was to get into the living room and grab those two guys. That would free Moe from the threat.

They exited the car and put their plan in motion. Everything worked fine until they arrived in the kitchen. They did not expect one of the gentleman to be at the sink getting a glass of water. When they open the kitchen door he turn and fired at Chucky. Chucky ducked and he missed him. The bullet went into the drywall. Jack pulled his gun out and shot the guy right between the eyes. He fell to his death at the sinks side. The other man took his gun off Moe's head and ran down the hallway to help his partner.

Moe took after him and leaped on his back. He grabbed him by the neck and they both fell to the floor. Moe began beating on this guys head. He beat him bloody. The man was motionless as Moe began swearing at him in Spanish.

Jack pulled Moe off him and helped him stand. The man was lying in his own blood. Moe turned and kicked him in the head behind the ear. That blow to killed him instantly.

"Ain't no thing! Don't let it trouble your Moe." Jack said.

"What are we gonna do with these two guys?" Moe replied.

"Throw them in the trunk I'll take them over to the sanitary canal. There's a place that we can dump them . We can tie a bolder to their backs and dump them in to the canal. They will go right to the bottom in the mud. They'll never be found after that." Jack told him.

"Great idea! Let's get this over with!" Moe said.

"Where is my money Moe?" Jack asked.

"I have it right in the front room . Moe walked into the front room and grab the bag next to the couch. He walked back and handed it to Jack.

"It's all there Jack if you want to count it. Moe told him.

"I believe you. I didn't think you would short me. If you did you would be going to the canal with those guys. Jack stuffed the sack in his back pocket. They hauled the bodies out to the car. Chucky had gone to bring the car to the back of the house.

Shortly after the corpses were loaded into the trunk Jack told Moe to go to Home Depot. Moe was instructed to get to 50 pound bags of cement. He was to meet them back at the canal.

The cement was to be wrapped into plastic and tied

on their backs. The bags would get wet and the cement would harden. That alone would sink the bodies to the bottom of the canal. Moe meet them and the task was completed. It worked as planned. They left and went their separate ways.

(ActV111). It took them several hours to purchase some crack. They waited around the drug house to meet the dealer. Going to buy crack is a real experience. The dealers tells you that he'll be there in 15 minutes and he don't show for another hour or two. What you do is sit, wait and call. They will just do nothing but lie to you but they do come thru.

Once they're arrive you pay them their money and make the exchange. This is what Chucky and Jack did and scored a $500 bag. They took it back to the trailer. Chucky invited a few friends by phone to come over and party with them.

There was going to be a real blow out. The party began as the first pipe was lit by Chucky. Once he took a hit the devil entered the trailer. Every crack head will tell you crack attracts Satan. Satan will make the house shake and everyone will become paranoid. You could be sitting on the couch next to your friend and you'll hear voices or imagine people coming and going. You will hear demons walking on the roof or outside the room. Crack is a real experience. If you're not ready for it you'll get the hell scared out of you.

They were four men on a binge . Several days had passed and they were still banging crack. Jack and Chucky spent $1300. The morning of the fifth day a gentleman came to the door.

He was a friend of another man that was inside. That other gentleman invited him in. Jack hated this guy's guts. Their friend smoked a pipe with him and he got high. He started saying things to Jack which upset him.

Jack became very riled and stood up. He grab the man by

the neck and beat his face with his fist. He didn't know this guy had a shank in his pocket. While Jack was punching him he reached down inside his pocket and grabbed hold of it.

He stabbed Jack right in the back. It killed him instantly and Jack fell to the floor. The blood began flowing all over the floor. All the crack heads ran out the door except Chucky. He was the only one left there. The neighbors in the campground heard the confusion and called the police. They ran out the door the police nabbed them.

The police entered the house and noticed Jack's body laying on the floor. Everyone was arrested including Chucky. They were brought down to the police station and interrogated.

After several hours of questioning one of the gentleman cracked the case wide-open for the police department. It was a friend of Moe's that had been in the house with them during the other shooting.

That friend came forward and told the police that Moe and two gentleman shot the men in the kitchen. He informed the police that the two gentlemen were holding guns at Moe's head. This happened in the front room before they were murdered. The snitch couldn't provide information but didn't how or who disposed of the bodies. He told them he ran from the house once the Murders happened. He didn't wanna stick around and get arrested.

The police called Moe and Chuck into the interrogation room. They were brought up in handcuffs and sat on a bench against a wall. They interrogated them for three hours in regards to the death of the two gentlemen. The police found out all the pertinent information including their names.

Chucky told them that he was only protecting Moe. Jack and him had seen them thru a window. The men were pointing a gun at Moe towards his head.

They came in through the basement door and up into the kitchen. They had to stop the abduction. The first shot was fired by one of the gentleman towards Chucky.

The second one was fired by Jack towards the gentleman and it hit him. He fell to the floor in front of the sink. The second man got beat up by Moe. He was kicked in the head and died instantly.

The police went back to the campground. The area surrounding the trailer was taped off by the police. There were crime investigators inside taking fingerprints and taking pictures. They had the evidence they needed against the men. They found a pound of cocaine and crack under the bedding. A storage area by the hot water tank was a hiding place.

In the distance came a tow truck and flatbed into the campground. The driver hooked up to the trailer and pulled it out. It was brought to the police impound along with Jacks car.

The police did a thorough check of Jack's car. They ran the license plate number state to state. They found out there was a APB issued for the car in Moline Illinois. There was also a description of Jack as he was wanted for an investigation of murder. The story was starting to come out.

They brought Chucky into the room again. He was asked if he came from Moline with Jack. Chuck couldn't lie and he admitted the truth.

Chuck was charged with the Murder and possession of illegal substance. He was being held at the state penitentiary.

Chucky had to go back to Moline and face the charge of a double Murder. Witnesses told them that Jack and Chucky picked up the two girls on the strip. That's how Chucky was implicated.

He wouldn't be transport to Moline until the trial was over up north. Chucky would have to serve his time for the crimes up north. Then he would be transferred to Moline after he served his sentence for the felonies.

The money that Jack and Chucky had been paid was in a bag. The police found it in the trailer by the sink. They confiscated the money until Chucky could explain where It came from. Two police officers drove to the penitentiary to question him about it.

They went into the warden's office and told them to bring Chucky to the interrogation quarters. Chucky was brought in and the questioning began.

Chucky had no information for the officers. He refused to tell them anything about the money. He knew that if he opened his mouth the thrill killers would murder him. He was in the same penitentiary they were in and on the same cell block.

It was very dangerous for Chucky just being in there with them. There were three other inmates that were arrested with him that we're on the same floor. All these inmates were together and there was tension. The thrill killers threatened Chucky. If he said one word they were going to murder him right in his cell.

Chucky was not the type person to be intimidated very easily. The thrill killers were a threat to him but he wasn't scared of them. He knew that Jack was not at his side to help. He was to face this alone without the help of a side kick.

The thrill killers weren't going to give him a chance to open his mouth. They were planning a hit. While out in the courtyard during recreation they met. The thrill killers and two men. The same two men that were arrested with Chucky.

The plan was put into place to kill him. They were going to do it in two days. They had to wait till one of the inmates made a shank in the kitchen. He worked in the dining room and was able to have access to knives.

The gentleman worked for those two days sharpening

that knife against a stone in the recreation yard. Once the shank was able to penetrate flesh he alerted the thrill killers.

The plan was to kill Chucky in the shower. They were going to stab him while he was washing.
The inmates were allowed showers daily. The four men kept an eye on Chucky. They needed to follow hIm when he enter the bath area. It's been

a long day and Chuck just came in from working out.

Chuckie had quite an extensive work out during the last hour. He was sweating from head to foot. He went to his bunk area and grabbed a towel and his toiletries.

He put on his shower shoes and walked up to the shower area. It was located just behind the guard station. The guards watched him walk in and they marked him in. The guards kept tract of inmates going in and out of the John.

He was in the shower about 11 minutes and Frank another inmate went in. There were eight showers lined up against one wall. It was one big open area. The showers were against a wall dividing them from the urinals and toilets. From the other side of the wall the inmates couldn't be seen by the guards.

Frank walked in with the shank rolled up in his towel. He went into the shower area and put his toiletries on the bench. He didn't expect Chucky to be on alert. He knew the thrill killers had a hit on him.

A strange feeling came over Chuckie about Frank. He knew that he wasn't safe and he was preparing an attack.

There is one thing Frank didn't know. Chucky wasn't stupid

and he had a shank of his own inside his shampoo bottle. Chucky continued washing and rinsed off. He was rinsing out the shampoo from his hair an seen Frankie approaching. He was coming up in behind him.

Chucky slowly opened the shampoo bottle and took his shank out. It was plastic and he made it out in the recreation yard. He turned swiftly as Frankie had the shank up in the air. He was prepared to stab him. Chucky turned and put his shank right in his abdomen. He pulled back and reinserted a second time.

Frankie fell to the floor with the shank in his gut. There was blood all over the floor. He ran out around the wall and told someone to get the guards. The guards came in and grabbed him. Chuckie started explaining what happened.

They still had to send him to lock up. They put the handcuffs on him and brought him down the stairs into isolation.

He was naked under a towel that loosely surrounded his waist. The officers went upstairs to his bed area and gathered his belongings. They brought all his clothes and personal things down to the isolation room where Chucky was being quarantined.

Chucky sat in that isolation room for about five weeks before he was taken to trial. He had a hearing in front of a board in regards to the murder. Chucky was able to free himself from the charges. He told him it was self-defense. He was only charge for the shank. Chucky server an extra year for having the shank. The murder charges were dropped for lack of evidence.

Chucky has completed all his court dates that were ahead of him. He had a total sentence of 13 years. He was to remain in the same penitentiary for the duration of the sentence

During his incarceration the police stumble on a news story about the barge. Evidently the barge hit the a wall and the side was damaged.

The barge was returned up north and docked in Moline. The barge was lifted and there were metal boxes welded to the bottom. After further investigation they discovered three bodies.

The bodies were deteriorated. All the skin was gone and there was nothing but bone remaining. The police have a hard job ahead of them. They had to find out who the bodies belong too. They were going through the missing persons reports.

They stumbled across the Black brothers. There was a story in the paper about them disappearing a few years ago. There grandmother had made a report and the police never found them.

The police were positive they solve the disappearance of the Black brothers. But who is the other man in the third coffin? They researched the missing persons reports further. They came across a few people that it could be but they couldn't identify them.

They were stumbled on the last one. The autopsy report on the bones show confirmed that the remains were definitely the Black Brothers. The remains were sent back to Indianapolis and the grandmother buried them. The police never identified the third person.

An Investigation was open on the Black brothers Murders. It was a year and a half and couldn't find out anything else about. All they knew was the brothers came looking for Amy Black. They went back into the Las Vegas files and couldn't locate any more information. The case went cold and the Murders were never found.

The police knew that the corpses had suffered a horrible death. Both of the bodies were decapitated. They found the skull laying on top of the stomach area of the skeleton. This was a terrible homicide the police determined.

It was six months later a prostitute from the river walk came forward. She told the police she had witnessed Jack and Chucky abduct one of the ladies. She admitted that during that time Caroline came to her an told her of the plan.

This opened a whole new look to the case. The police knew that Chuckie was involved in the Murder of these two men. He was also being investigating for the Murder of the Prostitute.

Chucky was pressed further and interrogated. He was facing three more charges of murder.

His trail date came and went quickly. He was found guilty of all three Murders. He had three lifetime sentences to serve.

During the court proceedings a questions came up about the thrill killers. Shawns name was mentioned in the procedure. The court found out that the thrill killers had hired Chuckie and Jack commit the Murders . The state police went and picked up the two of them from the penitentiary. They were brought to Moline to stand trial. They were convicted and now serving a life sentence. Ryan the shipyard worker was never charged.

                    The End

I hope you enjoyed the story. We have reached the conclusion of "The Floating Cemetery". You can see the tittle matched the manuscript.

I came up with the idea of the metal coffins under the barge while I was writing the story. I loved it and it inspired me to use them in the book.

My thoughts developed the circumstance that led up to the murders. I really enjoyed writing this book and describing three imaginary murders. I knew it would stun my readers.Thank You.

Books by: John S. Sylvester

Murder in Franklin County

Murder in Clark County Las Vegas " Condemned"

Case Of Amy Black

Call The Thrill Killers

Made in the USA
Monee, IL
18 April 2023